A SOLVE-THE-STORY PUZZLE ADVENTURE

PUZZLOO!ES

T0332090

WELCOME TO ESCAPE CITY

BY JONATHAN MAIER AND RUSSELL GINNS
ILLUSTRATED BY NATE BEAR

Visit us on the web! **rhcbooks.com**
For a variety of teaching tools, educators and librarians can visit us
at **RHTeachersLibrarians.com**.

ISBN: 978-0-525-57218-3 (trade paperback)

Cover design by Igor Jovicic
Cover art and interior illustration by Nate Bear
Interior design by Nicolette Cantillo

Printed in the United States of America

10 9 8 7 6 5 4 3 2 1

First Edition

What's a Puzzlooey?

Puzzlooies are stories you read by solving puzzles.

They're smart, surprising, and seriously silly.

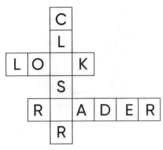

Each amazing adventure is chock-full of challenges, perplexing pictures, and mysterious messages. Plus there's always an extra helping of hilarious jokes and fascinating facts!

Let these zany, brainy kids introduce you to the story. They might even help with a clue or two. Start reading and puzzling. It's all up to you!

Eunice   **Maralee**

Ray   **Clinton**

How to Solve This Story

DETAIL DETECTOR

Every Puzzlooey is told through a mix of chapters and puzzles. To solve it all, you'll have to pay attention to many of the things you discover along the way.

PUZZLES ARE...

A-MAZE-ING!

CLUE COLLECTOR

You'll need a few things to make the most of this book:

- A pencil
- Scissors
- A ruler

PUZZLER PROPS

HINT: READ THE FIRST LETTER OF EACH BOLD WORD

Most of all, you'll need to use your **brunch roosters** and **island needlepoint.**

(Psst: If you get stuck, the answers are at the back.)

There's No Escape!

This story is a-**maze**-ing. A team makes a detour into a town, and they discover it's not so easy to get out.

You'll want to keep your pencil very **clues** to you, as all good fact **checkers** do.

Lost but not least, if you're **wandering** what this is all about. . .

WELCOME TO ESCAPE CITY

   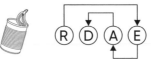

 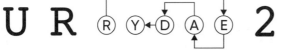

WON AND LOST

Tinsley Termites, we're the pros!
King our checkers, jump our foes!
Wipe their pieces off the board!
A giant trophy's our reward!

Sophie Stutts sat in the front seat of the charter bus and listened to the members of the checkers team chant at the top of their lungs. The Tinsley Termites were celebrating their first place win in the National Middle School Checkers Championship. They hadn't stopped yelling since the start of the long trip back home.

Sophie smiled to herself. In her own small way, she was part of their success.

The bus driver's brown eyes caught Sophie's gaze in the rearview mirror.

She spoke to Sophie over the chanting. "How come you're not back there whooping it up with the rest of your team?" As the driver talked, the tight bun at the back of her head bobbed up and down.

"Oh, I'm not really on the team," Sophie said. "I'm just the water captain. I'll go back there if they need me."

As if on cue, one of the kids shouted, "Stutts! Water me!"

Sophie popped up with a grin. "They need me!"

She hefted two water carriers, six bottles in each, and lugged them down the aisle of the bus. The carriers knocked against the seats. And several elbows.

With every collision, the team let her know about it: "Ouch!" "Hey, watch where you're going, Clumsy!" "Careful— that's my checker- jumping arm!"

Lyla Brackenbush, the one who'd originally ordered the water, yelled at Sophie. "Hurry up! I'm about to die of thirst here!"

When Sophie arrived, she pulled out the bottle labeled with Lyla's name and held the curved straw to the girl's lips. Sophie gave the bottle a gentle squeeze. Lyla greedily gulped down the water, then squeezed the bottle herself. Hard.

Lyla choked. Water exploded from her mouth. She doubled up in a fit of coughing.

Two seats back, the team's coach, Mr. Drilling, spoke sharply, "Stutts! You trying to drown our best player?"

"Wouldn't dream of it, Coach," Sophie said, then turned to Lyla. "You okay? Can I help?"

Lyla, her face red and scowling, waved Sophie away with the back of her hand.

When Sophie returned to her seat, the driver met her gaze in the rearview mirror once again. "Why don't you play checkers instead of toting their water around?"

Sophie shrugged. "Checkers isn't my thing," she said.

"What is your thing?"

"Besides water captain?" Sophie thought for a moment. "I don't know," she admitted. "I guess I'm waiting to find out."

The driver nodded. "Beep."

"I'm sorry," Sophie said. "What did you say?"

"Excuse me—hiccups," the driver explained. "I meant to say, 'Be patient.'"

Sophie smiled at hearing the advice.

The driver said, "My name's Mae, by the way. Mae Sheen."

Sophie introduced herself as well.

"Now that we've officially met," Mae said, "I have a confession: We're lost. I took a wrong turn somewhere, and there's no phone signal out here."

Out the side windows, rocks and patches of dry brush dotted a desert landscape. Straight ahead, a towering concrete wall stretched across the horizon, its surface etched with an intricate maze pattern. Arching above the wall's only entrance, a sign read: WELCOME TO ESCAPE CITY.

"Maybe somebody there can help us," Mae said as she drove through the entrance.

Mae drove slowly through the city streets, circling a central plaza.

Sophie narrowed her eyes. "Something's weird here."

1 RIDE & READ

Start at the arrow and follow the main path. Read the letters as you go to find out what's weird about the city.

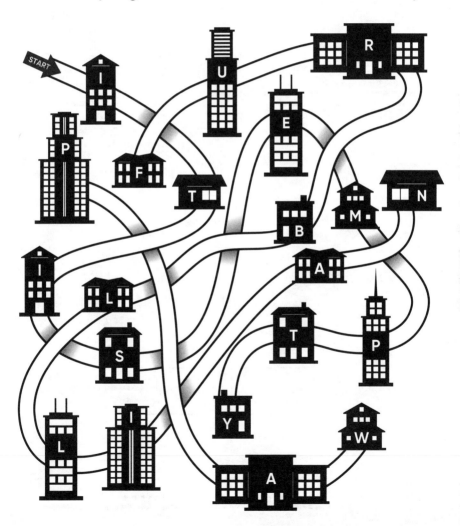

WRITE YOUR ANSWER ON THE NEXT PAGE

WRITE YOUR ANSWER

___ ___   ___ ___

___ ___ ___ ___ ___

"There's nobody in this city," Sophie said.
Suddenly, a loud noise sounded from behind the bus.
Everyone spun around to see what had happened.

Write all of these words in alphabetical order on the back of this page. The letters in shaded boxes will spell what all the commotion is about.

R U M B L E

K A B O O M

Z I N G

C R A S H

T H U D

P L O P

W H I R

C R E A K

WRITE YOUR ANSWERS ON THE NEXT PAGE

WRITE YOUR ANSWERS

Massive steel doors had swung shut and sealed the entrance. A deep voice thundered from every direction. "Attention!" it began.

Start with the Y then read every THIRD letter. Keep going around until you've used all the letters to find out what the voice said.

WRITE YOUR ANSWER ON THE NEXT PAGE

WRITE YOUR ANSWER

___ ___ ___   ___ ___ ___ ___

___ ___ ___   ___ ___ ___ ___ ___

___ ___   ___ ___ ___ ___ ___ ___

AN UNLOCK-Y NUMBER

"Two hours to escape?" Lyla said. She—as well as every other Tinsley Termite—looked at Coach Drilling with big eyes. "What happens if we don't?"

Drilling took off his ball cap and scratched his head. "I have no idea."

He walked to the front of the bus and asked Mae, "Where are we?"

"Sorry, sir," Mae said. "I'm afraid we're lost."

Drilling had Mae park next to the plaza and everyone cleared out of the bus. All eyes turned to a tall stone statue at the center of the empty plaza. It was a stack of twenty small dogs standing on each other's backs. A digital clock rested on the top dog. It read, "1:59."

"That's the wrong time," Drilling said.

Standing at his elbow, Sophie said, "Um, I don't think it's a clock, Coach. It's a timer counting down."

Sure enough, the readout changed to "1:58." A few kids tried to phone for help, but discovered they had no signal. The checkers team moaned and whimpered. They were starting to panic.

Coach Drilling blew his whistle. Everyone jumped.

"Get a grip!" he snapped. "We're the Tinsley Termites Checkers Team. Nobody's better! Nobody's smarter! Escape City is just another opponent we're gonna take down!"

The team spontaneously started to chant: "Tinsley Termites, we're the pros!"

"Coach!" Titus Spackler said. He was the second-best player on the team. "I found a clue!"

He pointed behind them to the closed entrance doors. Painted across them in bold letters was the question: IF YOU KNOW WHERE TWO GO, THEN WHAT ARE YOU WEIGHTING FOUR?

Everybody gathered in front of the doors and studied the words.

"Whoever wrote it can't spell," Lyla said. "It's full of mistakes."

Sophie, who stood behind her, quietly said, "I think all the misspellings are numbers."

"Numbers!" Lyla announced. "The question has hidden numbers! Two, eight, and four."

"Great work, Lyla," Coach Drilling said. "It must be a code."

"For sure, to this combination lock." Titus smirked and patted a dial attached to the wall next to the doors. It was as big as a tractor tire and circled with numbers.

Team members rushed to the dial and clamored to turn it. Sophie and Mae stood at a distance while twenty kids pawed at the lock and yelled at each other.

"Focus, Termites!" Drilling said, "Begin with number two."

Sophie didn't think escaping could be as easy as opening a single lock. *The numbers must be for something else*, she thought.

She studied the grand buildings that lined three sides of the plaza. As she took in their marble columns and impressive staircases, a movement caught her eye. A small white dog bolted up the steps of the building marked CITY HALL. When it reached the top, it nudged its way through the main doors. Above the doors, in gold letters, the building address read 284.

Sophie turned to Mae. "I saw a dog! Like the ones in the statue."

Mae looked around. "Are you sure?"

"Pretty sure," Sophie said, "and I think I know where the clue points to. Can you come check with me? If I'm right we can let the team know."

Mae agreed. As they rushed across the plaza to the City Hall steps, something went *KA-CHUNK!*

"We opened the lock! We're free!" the checkers team shouted.

But the giant steel doors didn't open. Instead, everything began to rumble. A sheet of curved glass rose from the surrounding walls. It slid over the city like a snow globe, trapping everyone inside. Only a single small hole at the top of the dome provided an opening to the outside.

The checkers team started to scream for help while Drilling blasted his whistle.

"Oh dear," Sophie said. "I hope I'm right about this." She and Mae climbed the steps and entered City Hall.

City Hall was just that: an empty hall with four unmarked doors.

"I guess we'll have to try all of them," Sophie said.

4 HALL OR NOTHING

Find out which door leads to the way out.

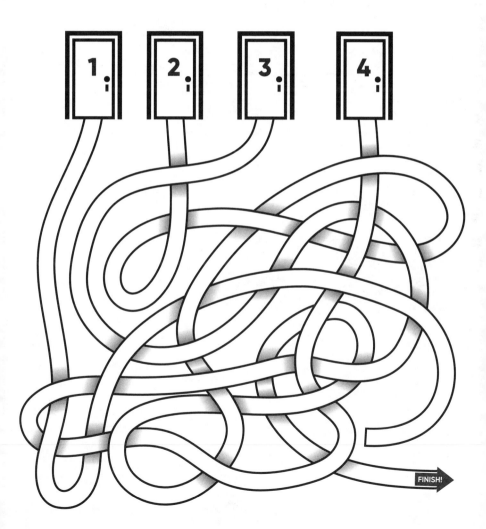

They entered an empty room with only a single window that looked out at a tall building across the street.

Now what do we do? Sophie wondered.

Tilt this page back until you can read a word.
Then turn it sideways and tilt it to read another word.
You'll discover what Sophie should try next.

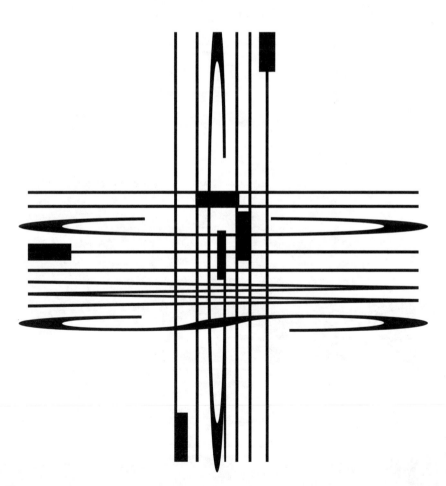

When Sophie flicked on the light switch, a letter lit up in each window of the building across the street.

"Whoa! A giant word search," Sophie said.

Find all the building parts hidden in this word search, including diagonally and backwards. (There's a list of them on the back of this page.) The leftover letters will spell out the next clue.

C	H	I	M	N	E	Y	S
O	S	R	O	O	L	F	E
N	G	S	T	A	I	R	S
C	N	P	A	I	N	T	S
R	I	T	I	L	E	I	T
E	N	O	T	S	G	A	E
T	W	O	D	N	I	W	E
E	A	L	F	O	O	R	L

——— ——— ——— ———

LOOK HERE FOR LIST OF SEARCH WORDS

SEARCH WORDS

AWNING	PAINT	STONE
CHIMNEY	ROOF	TILE
CONCRETE	SIGN	WINDOW
FLOORS	STAIRS	
GLASS	STEEL	

"The leftover words spell SEAL," Sophie said.

"Like the…" Mae slapped her hands together several times and barked. *"Ark! Ark! Ark!"*

"You do a great seal," Sophie said. "But I don't see one around here."

As soon as she said it, though, she realized she was wrong. Hanging on the opposite wall was a large round plaque.

"A *city* seal!" Sophie realized.

Mae patted her on the back. "Beep!"

"Hiccups, again?" Sophie asked.

Mae smiled sheepishly. "I was going to say, 'Be proud of yourself!'"

In the center of the seal, a dog held a lock and key. *Getting free is the key*, the seal read.

On a hunch, Sophie went to the plaque, pinched the raised form of the key, and gave it a tug. It pulled out!

Sophie happily waved the key in front of Mae, who grinned and clapped. Then Sophie tried inserting the key in the dog's lock. It fit perfectly. Her chest tightened a bit as she gave the key a twist.

The room groaned. The floor trembled. Sophie and Mae dropped onto their hands and knees for stability. The entire room started to lift. The view through the window disappeared behind a scrolling brick wall.

"The room is an elevator!" Sophie shouted.

A minute later, the room stopped with a *CLUNK*.

The doorway slid open. Cautiously, Sophie and Mae stood up and stepped through it. They were on a patio at the top of the building. Silver platters, piled high with wrapped hamburgers, covered two long tables.

"Wow, there's enough burgers here for the whole team," Sophie said. "I think it's time we went back and let them know we're on the right track."

But just then, the patio entrance slid shut behind them. No doorknob. No way back in. They were stuck outside, high walls on either side of them. The only open side looked over a railing to the street far below.

On the roof of the building across from them was a huge advertising billboard.

Sophie picked up a burger from the table. "Look— the wrapping has a lightbulb pattern. Bright Idea. Get it? Must be the same burgers as the sign." It smelled delicious, but Sophie felt too anxious to eat. She offered the hamburger to Mae.

"No, thank you," Mae said. "I don't eat."

"You what?" Sophie stared at her with a raised eyebrow.

"I mean," Mae stammered, "I don't eat hamburgers."

"Oh. Okay." Sophie glanced at the sign again. "Wish *I* had a bright idea. Sorry I got us stuck up here, Mae. By now, the checkers team has probably found the real way out."

"The ones who sealed us in a dome?" Mae shook her head. "I don't think so. You're doing great, Sophie. All the clues led us here. Beep—excuse me—be persistent."

Mae is right, Sophie thought. She examined the burgers and the sign again. Maybe there was a connection. She was struck by the kid's words: "I could eat three of 'em!"

Huh, Sophie thought. *Maybe we should feed him.*

Sophie heaved the burger she was holding at the sign. It hit the kid in the eye and dropped onto the rooftop. She threw another, adjusting her aim. It dropped into the kid's mouth—the mouth was an opening!

The lights in the word BRIGHT flickered. Some of its letters flashed off, leaving only BR lit up. Sophie's next throw hit the mouth as well. IDEA flickered and left only ID lit up. It took two more throws until she hit the target the third time. Now the only letters lit up were:

BRIGHT IDEA BURGERS

"Bridge," Sophie read. At once, the letters disappeared, and the billboard tilted toward them. It slowly lowered over the street like a drawbridge and came to rest on the patio railing.

Sophie and Mae climbed onto the billboard bridge and walked to a door that led into the other building.

"I wonder what's inside," Sophie said.

Use the list of places and fit each word into the crossword. The letters in the shaded spaces will reveal where Sophie and Mae are headed next.

Bank
Dam
Gym
Kennel
Library
Museum
School
Theater
Zoo

___ ___ ___ ___

As they searched the mall for clues, Sophie noticed something odd about the store signs.

"Some of the words are scrambled," she said.

Unscramble the underlined word on each store sign. Then use the highlighted letters to spell the next clue.

Furry Friends **SEPT** ___ ___ ___ ___

Gold and
Silver **JRLEWEY** ___ ___ ___ ___ ___ ___ ___

Sweet Treat
DACYN ___ ___ ___ ___ ___

For Kicks **ESSOH** ___ ___ ___ ___ ___

Playmaker
STROSP ___ ___ ___ ___ ___ ___

Wear 'Em
CETHOLS ___ ___ ___ ___ ___ ___ ___

Page-Turner
SOBOK ___ ___ ___ ___ ___

**WRITE YOUR ANSWER
ON THE NEXT PAGE**

WRITE YOUR ANSWER

___ ___ ___ ___

Sophie and Mae exited the mall to the street. Large traffic sign arrows pointed the way to the park.

Sophie smiled and shouted. "This way!"

Follow the direction of the arrows to find the path to the park. Note: You can't go through an arrow in the opposite direction.

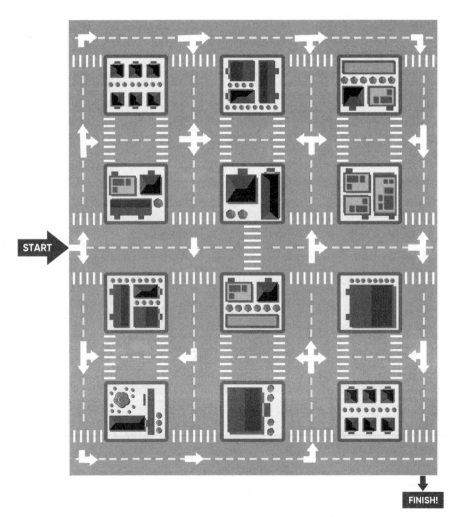

WATER WE GOING TO DO?

"We found it!" Sophie exclaimed.

At the corner of the intersection ahead stood a marble slab with the word PARK carved into its face. As Sophie and Mae arrived at the entrance, they heard kids shouting. The checkers team was already there.

Sophie knew she should be happy that they were okay and she'd finally met up with them. But instead, she felt a little disappointed that they'd gotten this far without her.

Her thoughts were interrupted by a clatter of metal. *CLANKITY-CLANKITY-CLACKITY!*

A galloping swing set charged toward her and Mae. Coach Drilling sat in the middle seat gripping its chains for dear life.

"Stop this thing!" he shrieked.

Sophie and Mae jumped out of the way before the swing set's legs could trample them. A whirling merry-go-round on wheels followed closely behind. Then came a crab-walking set of monkey bars. Screaming kids clung to the play structures as they careened into the street. More kids chased after the runaway structures on foot.

Sophie spotted Lyla Brackenbush in the group and stopped her. "What's happening?"

"What's it look like, Stutts?" Lyla said with an eyeroll. "We're escaping. Obviously. We activated the robotic playground equipment, and now it's gonna lead us out of here. Come on!"

Lyla ran a few steps, then turned back. "And why don't you have our water bottles? It's your one job!" She rushed after the chaotic parade of kids and play structures.

"Should we follow them?" Mae asked Sophie.

Sophie grimaced as if she'd caught a whiff of stinky feet. "Nah," Sophie said. "I don't think they actually know what they're doing."

As Sophie led the way into the park, a white dog dashed across the path and into a thicket of bushes.

"Did you see that?" Sophie asked. "It's the dog again."

"Maybe it accidently wandered in here," Mae said. "Sort of like us."

"Maybe," Sophie said, but she didn't think so. She felt the dog had to be connected in some way with the dogs in the plaza statue and on the city seal.

She and Mae spent the next fifteen minutes searching the park for clues.

Mae checked her watch. "We have less than an hour to escape."

"Oh dear," Sophie sighed. "We've looked everywhere. Let's take a breather and think for a minute."

They sat on a bench that faced the park's central fountain, which was designed to look like a circle of oversized fire hydrants that shot water in every direction. Scattered across the fountain area were various water toys, including a bunch of brightly colored plastic buckets.

Sophie propped her head in her hands. *What are we going to do?* she thought.

A giant manhole cover was embedded in the cement in front of her. It was about six feet across and inscribed with a maze-like pattern. As she continued to examine it, she realized there were words woven into the pattern. They read: THE WEIGH OUT.

Sophie gasped. Weigh out. *Way* out.

"Mae, could you stand on this manhole cover with me?" Sophie asked, hopping to her feet.

Mae shrugged and joined Sophie on the metal circle. Ever so slightly, the cover sank into the ground.

"It's the 'weigh' out! Get it?" Sophie exclaimed. "But I think we need more weight." She looked around and spotted the array of plastic buckets.

"We can fill those buckets with water!" she said. "No problem for a water captain! Let's go!"

Mae hesitated. "I can't," she said.

"You can't? Is something wrong?" Sophie asked.

"I'm...um..." Mae glanced down, "...allergic to water."

"How can you be—?" But Sophie stopped herself. She felt it might be impolite to question it.

So, by herself, Sophie collected the water in buckets and set them down on the manhole cover. When she added the tenth bucket, the metal plate went *CLICK* and slowly lowered Sophie and Mae into the ground.

Sophie and Mae descended into an underground network of pipes and tunnels. Sophie was sure they could find a way under the city wall and get out.

10 PIPE DOWN!

Find a path that could lead Sophie and Mae out of the city.

START

FINISH!

The maze of tunnels ended at a flight of stairs.

"We did it…I hope!" Sophie charged up the steps and through the exit. But then she stopped, confused.

Start at HOPE and make new words by changing one letter at a time. The last word will reveal where Sophie and Mae are.

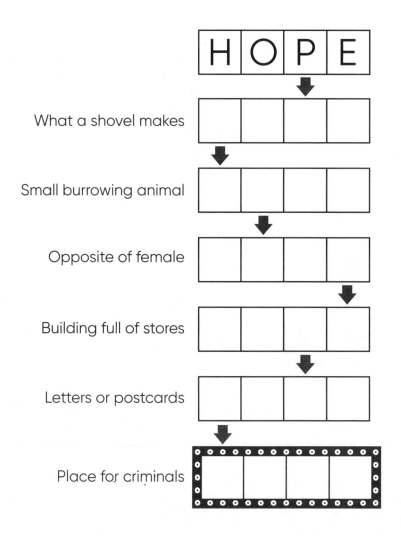

	HOPE
What a shovel makes	
Small burrowing animal	
Opposite of female	
Building full of stores	
Letters or postcards	
Place for criminals	

As Mae joined Sophie, the exit door slammed behind them. They were in a jail cell! But they weren't alone. Across the corridor was another occupied cell.

With a ruler, draw five vertical lines to connect the cell bars. The leftover letters will reveal who else was in jail.

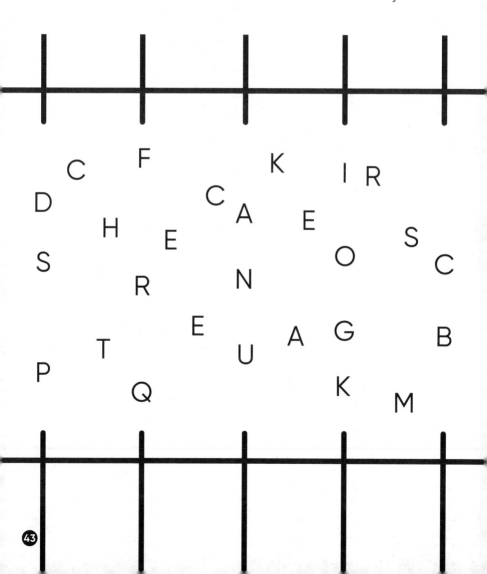

Nobody gets all the way through a Puzzlooey without encountering a collection of...

Amazing Facts

Marion Franklin Tinsley (1927–1995), considered the greatest professional checkers player of all time, lost fewer than 10 games in 45 years.

In 1994, a computer program became the checkers World champion.

The world's largest jigsaw puzzle for sale has 51,300 pieces. It takes about 20 days to complete, working full-time.

Word searches first appeared printed in newspapers and magazines in the 1960s.

There are 500,000,000,000,000,000,000 (500 quintillion) different combinations of moves that can be made in a game of checkers.

The first crossword puzzle appeared in the *New York World* newspaper on December 21, 1913. The creator called it a "word cross puzzle."

A person who makes or solves crossword puzzles is called a cruciverbalist.

The most people who played checkers at the same time in one place is 540 in Reno, Nevada, in 2014.

In 2011 in Latvia, 88 people set the world record for the most people to play checkers underwater at the same time.

Ernő Rubik invented the Rubik's Cube in Hungary in 1974. Since then, more the 450 million of them have been sold worldwide.

Of course, it wouldn't be an official, mysterious, escape-proof Puzzlooey if it didn't include...

Riddles and Jokes

Q: How did the ice cube escape from the freezer?
A: With a well-thawed-out plan.

Q: What's the worst part about being a bus driver?
A: Everyone talks behind your back.

Q: What are you when you're tired of playing games?
A: Checkerbored.

Q: Why did the chicken cross the playground?
A: To get to the other slide.

Q: Why were all the clues dizzy?
A: They were in a whirred search.

Q: What do farm animals do to relax?
A: Pig-saw puzzles.

Q: Where does the crossword maker live?
A: Her street's three across and two down.

Q: Why was the jigsaw puzzle sad at the school dance?
A: He just didn't fit in.

Q: Why did the painting go to jail?
A: It was framed.

Knock-knock!
Who's there?
Mikey
Mikey who?
Mikey doesn't fit the lock!

We now return to **WELCOME TO ESCAPE CITY**

The checkers team pointed at Sophie through the bars of their jail cell and howled with laughter.

"This is what you get for not following us!" Lyla called out to Sophie.

Sophie didn't bother to point out that they were in the exact same situation.

The cells were big—bigger even than Sophie's living room back home. Vertical bars lined the front with a cell door in the middle. The rest were windowless brick walls. Sophie tested the door. It was locked tight.

"What'd you think?" Titus Spackler said. "You were gonna just walk out of here?"

Lyla said, "We've already tried everything. If *we* can't figure it out, you *never* will."

Coach Drilling shushed her. "We're not giving up, people! Remember, we're Tinsley Termites!"

He started the team chant, but nobody joined in.

Sophie turned to Mae with slumped shoulders. "Maybe Lyla's right. If the national middle school checkers champions can't find a way out, what chance do we have?"

"Trust yourself, Sophie," Mae said, placing a hand on the girl's shoulder. "You have a real talent for solving puzzles. Look how far you've gotten us."

"I am looking," Sophie said glumly. "We're in prison."

Despite her doubts, Sophie scanned the room for anything that might help them. Above her head, a small plastic star hung like a tree ornament from the ceiling light. It flashed and twinkled.

Curious, Sophie thought, but she had no idea what it could mean.

And then she spotted something she'd missed at first glance. It was hooked on one of the cell's crossbars and the same color metal: a crowbar!

Sophie grabbed it, thrust it over her head, and announced, "Look what I found!"

"Whoop-de-doo," Lyla said with a sneer. She gestured with her thumb at Titus, who had a crowbar hooked in the back of his pants like a tail. He was trying to crack up his teammates by pretending to be a monkey. Nobody laughed.

"We have one too," Lyla said. "And we already tried it on the bars. Nothing budged."

Discouraged, Sophie lowered the crowbar. She'd been so sure it was the key to breaking out.

One of the kids whined, "There's only a half-hour left!"

"We're goners!" Titus wailed. "You know what happens in the movies? When the timer runs out, everything blows up!"

He grabbed the crowbar from his pants and dragged it back and forth over the cell bars. "Help! Let me out! I don't want to explode!"

All the kids started shouting, but Sophie tuned them out. She was focused on another sound: the crowbar against the cell bars. It sounded musical, like someone playing scales on a xylophone. *The bars made different notes!*

She tapped a few of the cell bars with her own crowbar. Again, different notes.

"Mae, I think we're supposed to play a tune," Sophie said.

"What tune?" Mae asked.

"I don't have a clue," Sophie said. "Wait! I *do* have a clue."

She looked at the star hanging above them. The twinkling star.

Sophie wasn't talented musically, but she'd had a few piano lessons, enough to work out a simple tune. She began to pick out notes on the bars. It took her several tries, but eventually she played a clumsy verse of *Twinkle, Twinkle, Little Star*.

Her cell door swung open. The checkers team gasped.

"How did you do that?" Lyla said. "Now get us out!"

Sophie stepped out of her cell and played the same tune on their bars, but it had no effect.

"Try again!" Lyla shrieked.

Mae pulled Sophie aside. "No time. We have to go."

Sophie nodded. Somebody had to escape, and good as the team was at playing checkers, they were terrible at solving puzzles. But they were still her classmates, and she refused to be as mean as them.

"I'll get help!" Sophie promised and darted away before anyone could answer.

A door at the end of the corridor opened out onto the street. As Sophie's eyes adjusted to the sudden brightness, she began to make out a huge structure ahead.

1) Cross out all buildings with flat roofs.
2) Cross out all buildings with an odd number of windows.
The leftover letters will spell out what Sophie saw.

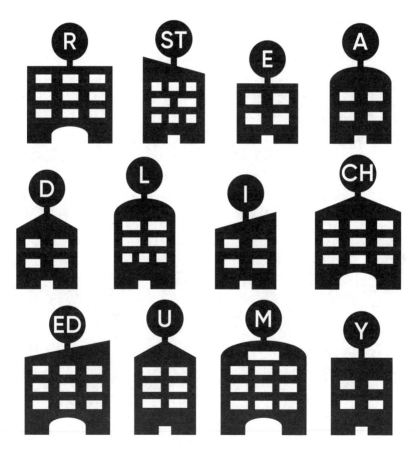

— — — — — — —

The marquee on the stadium was filled with a bunch of dog-related symbols.

"We're going to have to crack this code," Sophie said.

Use the guide at the bottom of this page to decipher the code and find out what the marquee says.

__ __ __

__ __ __ __ __

__ __ __ __

C   L   N   I   F   E   H   U   A   T

They hurried inside the stadium for the final clue.
Sophie stopped suddenly.

"That's not a football field!" she shouted.

Cut out the square. Then fold it on the dotted lines to make a smaller square that's all gray on one side and has all the letters on the other side. The letters will tell what Sophie saw.

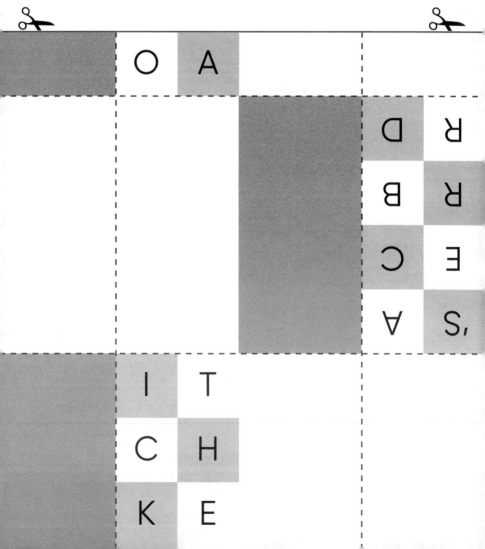

THE BIG GAME

Down on the field, surrounded by empty stadium stands, a huge checkerboard was set up for a match. Red and black checkers were placed in their starting positions at each end of the board.

"Who plays on this thing?" Sophie asked. "Giants? Mecha-robots?"

Mae smiled. "I'd like to see that."

"What do we do now?" Sophie asked. She looked for words and signs that might contain clues, or something that seemed out of place or unusual. But nothing was more unusual than the checkerboard.

She decided to take a closer look. Side by side, she and Mae descended the stadium steps.

"I've been wondering," Sophie said. "Why would someone build an escape room the size of a city? And how? Some of the stuff here doesn't seem possible."

"Oh, it's definitely possible," Mae replied. "We made sure that—I mean—*whoever* built this place must have had a reason for everything."

Sophie was about to ask Mae what she meant, but as she stepped onto the grass surrounding the checkerboard an announcer's voice began to blare.

"Our challenger has taken the field!"

Sophie stumbled and caught her breath.

"Challenger?" she asked. "What challenger?"

Mae stood at the railing just above the field.

"I think he means you," she called down to Sophie.

"But I don't play checkers," said Sophie. "I'm just the water captain."

"How many games have you watched?" Mae asked.

"Thousands," Sophie answered.

"I bet you've learned a thing or two," said Mae.

"Will you help me?" Sophie asked.

"Sorry, I don't know the rules," Mae said. "*Beep!*—excuse me—be positive."

OUR CHALLENGER!

"And here comes our champion!" the announcer called.

An invisible crowd roared from somewhere. Sophie stared across the field at the entrance tunnel. Several seconds passed before her opponent came trotting out into the sunlight.

It was the little white dog.

I'm playing against a dog? thought Sophie, confused.

"The rules are simple," the announcer said. "Every time the challenger jumps one of the champion's checkers, a letter of the final clue will be revealed on the stadium scoreboard. The champion goes first."

How am I going to move these checkers? Sophie wondered. *I'd need a forklift.*

As if to answer, the dog poked one of the checkers with its nose. The checker rose and hovered slightly off the ground. The dog nudged it one space forward.

Sophie took a deep breath. "I guess I'm doing this."

Time Out!

You're going to need all your puzzling power to solve this last challenge. And to answer all the questions, you might have to go back and check some of the facts you've encountered over the course of this story.

Ready, set. . .escape!

HINT:
The answer to the third question is on page 7.

YOU CAN DO IT!!

The white dog was the first to jump a checker. Sophie realized that if she lost too many checkers, she wouldn't discover the secret clue. She had to focus. *She had to win.*

16 JUMP TO A CONCLUSION

Complete all the questions. Then, read the letters in the checker's path to find out the final clue to escaping.

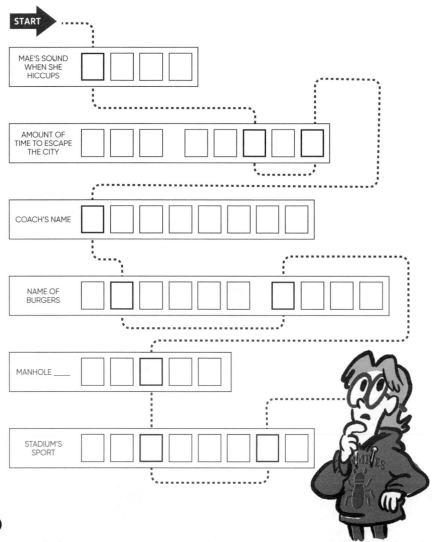

START

MAE'S SOUND WHEN SHE HICCUPS

AMOUNT OF TIME TO ESCAPE THE CITY

COACH'S NAME

NAME OF BURGERS

MANHOLE ____

STADIUM'S SPORT

GOING TO THE DOGS

With her last jump, not only did Sophie reveal the entire clue, but she also won the game. The dog had no moves left.

"We have a new champion!" the announcer declared. The invisible crowd went wild.

The white dog snorted and trotted back into the tunnel.

Sophie looked up at the scoreboard. The final clue was BUS DRIVER. She walked to where Mae had been watching from the stands.

"You're the final clue?" Sophie asked. As she thought about it, though, there were a lot of unusual things about Mae's behaviors. Sophie just hadn't put the pieces together. Until now.

"Yes," Mae said. "And you should know something about me. I'm—"

"A robot?" Sophie interrupted.

Mae blinked. "You knew?"

"Wait. Really?" Sophie had her hunches, but she was still shocked at the truth of it. "Well, you did say a lot of weird things, including that you don't eat. And you didn't want to get wet. And the beeping. Those weren't hiccups."

"Slight malfunctions," Mae sighed. "I need a tune-up."

"And just now I remembered your full name," Sophie said. "Mae Sheen. *Machine.* It was right in front of me the whole time."

"Of course, you figured it out." said Mae. "I'm sorry I couldn't tell you everything. but I knew you were capable of great things, which is why I brought you to Escape City."

Sophie had so many questions, but she could only watch in amazement as Mae reached behind her head and gave her hair bun a quarter turn. Her body transformed, bristling with metal and machinery. Flames shot from her feet. She rose into the air and stretched her arms to Sophie.

"Can I give you a lift?" Mae asked.

"Who-o-oa!" Sophie said, reeling back a step. "But, wait. What about the team? You're not going to blow them up are you? They can be super-annoying, but—"

"Time to go," Mae said and scooped Sophie up off the ground. They shot up to the small opening at the top of the dome.

With seconds to spare, Sophie landed just outside of the city entrance.

The bus was parked next to a small table where three white dogs seemed to be playing poker. When the dogs saw Sophie and Mae arrive, they dropped their cards and hopped onto their hind legs.

One of them said, "Congratulations on your escape, Sophie Stutts."

Sophie gasped. "You're the dog I played checkers with."

"No, Sophie Human. That was our pet dog, Fizzbit. She's very smart," the creature said. "We just look like dogs, but we're actually Furballians. We have come here from the planet Kibble Prime to find contestants."

"Contestants?" Sophie exclaimed. For what?"

"We run an interplanetary competition called *Welcome to Escape Planet*. And Sophie Human, because of your great puzzle-solving skill, we want you to represent Earth in the contest. You'll have a month to prepare, then we'll return in our ship to escort you to Kibble Prime."

"What ship?" Sophie said.

The Furballian pointed at the city.

"Escape City is a spaceship?" Sophie asked.

The three Furballians nodded, their tongues and tails wagging.

"But what about the Tinsley Termites checkers champs?" asked Sophie.

"Never fear, Sophie Human," one of them said. "The irritating team will join you shortly for the trip home. Then we'll come back for you to represent your planet."

Sophie took a deep breath. She felt thrilled and nervous all at once. *Represent all of Earth in an interplanetary puzzle contest?*

"If you like, I'll stay here with you," Mae told her. "I can help you train for the competition."

Sophie thought a moment. And smiled. Mae had believed in her the whole time. Now she was going to be her cosmic coach.

"That would *beep*!" said Sophie, taking hold of Mae's hand. "I mean, that would *be* perfect!"

Hooray for Puzzlooies!
Big, fun adventures for you.
Excitement and action
For you to peruse,
With a story in the middle
Of the riddles and clues.

You solved a Puzzlooey.
It's over, it's finished, it's through.
And if books about exits
Made you wonder what's next, it's...
Good that more are waiting for you!

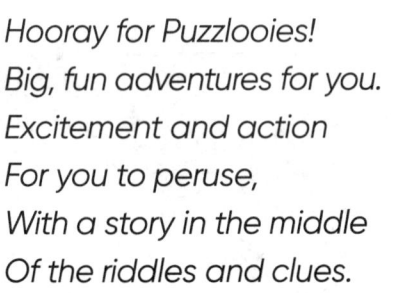

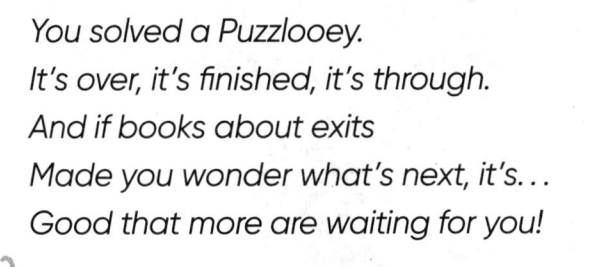

For more smart
and silly fun, go to
puzzlooies.com

ANSWERS

1 ## RIDE & READ

IT IS EMPTY

2 ## THE NOISE KNOWS

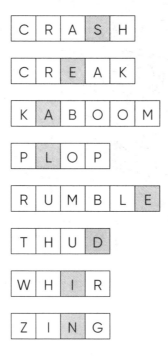

C R A **S** H

C R **E** A K

K **A** B O O M

P **L** O P

R U M B L **E**

T H U **D**

W H **I** R

Z **I** N G

SEALED IN

Great Work!

You riddled your way into town, and you puzzled your way out again.

Sophie and the rest of the team escaped, and it couldn't have happened without your brilliant brainpower and spectacular solving skills.

Now there isn't anything left to say, except...

3 TICK TALK

YOU HAVE TWO HOURS TO ESCAPE

4 HALL OR NOTHING

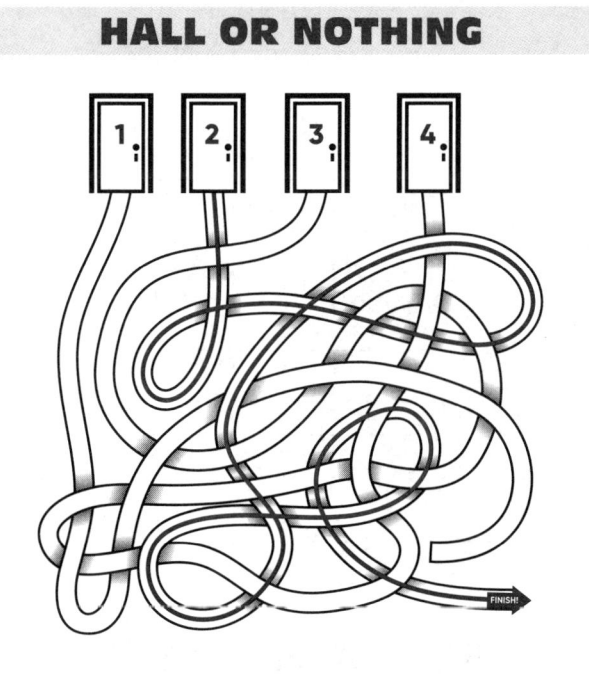

5 WORDS TO THE WISE

LIGHT SWITCH

SEAL

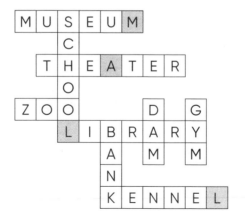

MALL

8 DIS-STORE-GANIZED

<u>P</u>ETS

<u>J</u>E<u>W</u>E<u>L</u>RY

<u>C</u>A<u>N</u>D<u>Y</u>

<u>S</u>H<u>O</u>E<u>S</u>

<u>S</u>P<u>O</u>R<u>T</u>S

<u>C</u>L<u>O</u>T<u>H</u>E<u>S</u>

<u>B</u>O<u>O</u>K<u>S</u>

PARK

9 DIRECTION DETECTION

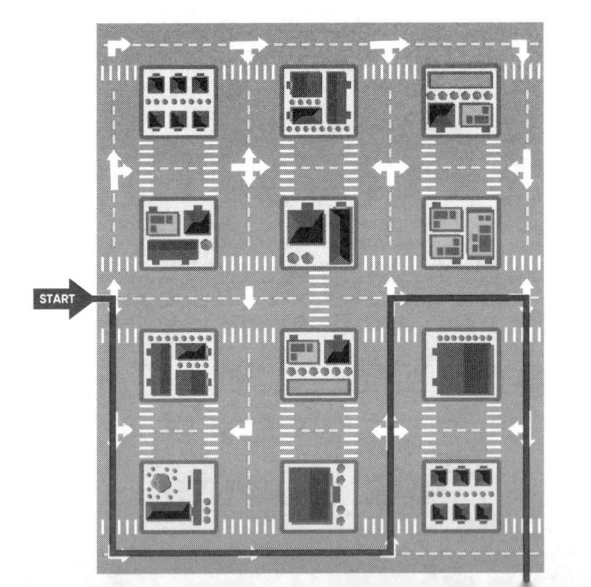

PIPE DOWN!

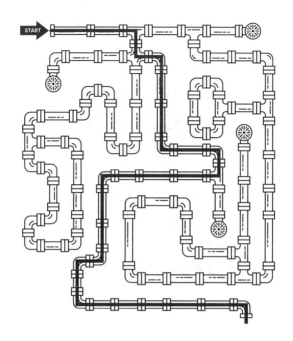

BEYOND HOPE

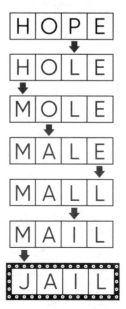

12   ## BEHIND BARS

CHECKERS TEAM

13   ## BUILDING INSPECTOR

STADIUM

14   ## CANINE CODE

THE FINAL CLUE

15   ## FOLD-A-FIELD

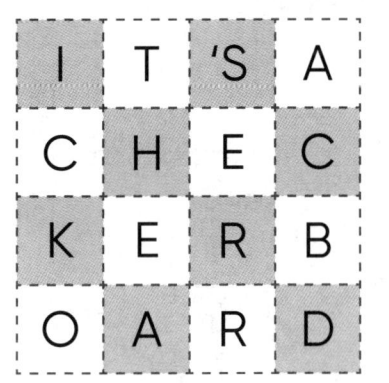

IT'S A CHECKERBOARD

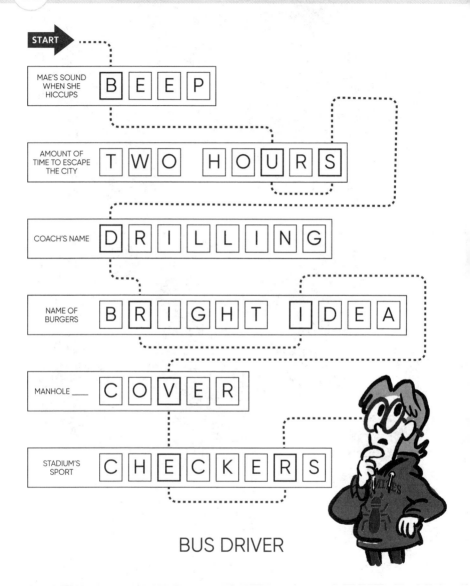

START

| MAE'S SOUND WHEN SHE HICCUPS | B | E | E | P |

| AMOUNT OF TIME TO ESCAPE THE CITY | T | W | O | | H | O | U | R | S |

| COACH'S NAME | D | R | I | L | L | I | N | G |

| NAME OF BURGERS | B | R | I | G | H | T | | I | D | E | A |

| MANHOLE ___ | C | O | V | E | R |

| STADIUM'S SPORT | C | H | E | C | K | E | R | S |

BUS DRIVER

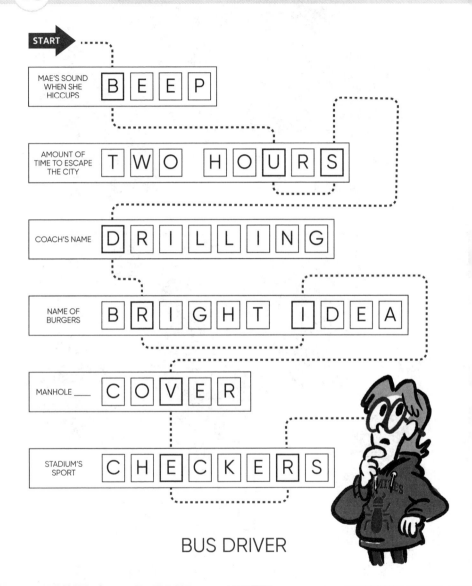

START

MAE'S SOUND
WHEN SHE
HICCUPS
B E E P

AMOUNT OF
TIME TO ESCAPE
THE CITY
T W O H O U R S

COACH'S NAME
D R I L L I N G

NAME OF
BURGERS
B R I G H T I D E A

MANHOLE ___
C O V E R

STADIUM'S
SPORT
C H E C K E R S

BUS DRIVER

THEY'RE SMART! THEY'RE FUNNY!
TELL YOUR PARENTS TO
GIVE YOU MONEY FOR MORE...

PUZZLOO!ES

COLLECT THEM ALL!

To learn more about the other zany, brainy adventures, visit:

PUZZLOOIES.COM